MW01142377

The Journey Home

STORY BY CAROL RAIKES
ILLUSTRATED BY J.W. RAIKES

SleepyGnome Publishing

For Misha and Ilia

Text copyright 2002 by Carol Raikes
Illustrations copyright 2002 by Jason Raikes
All rights reserved.

Published by Sleepy Gnome Publishing
A division of Robert Raikes, Inc., Tucson, AZ
www.raikes.com/sleepygnome/home.html

ISBN 0-9714253-1-0

Library of Congress Control Number: 2002090224

Printed in China

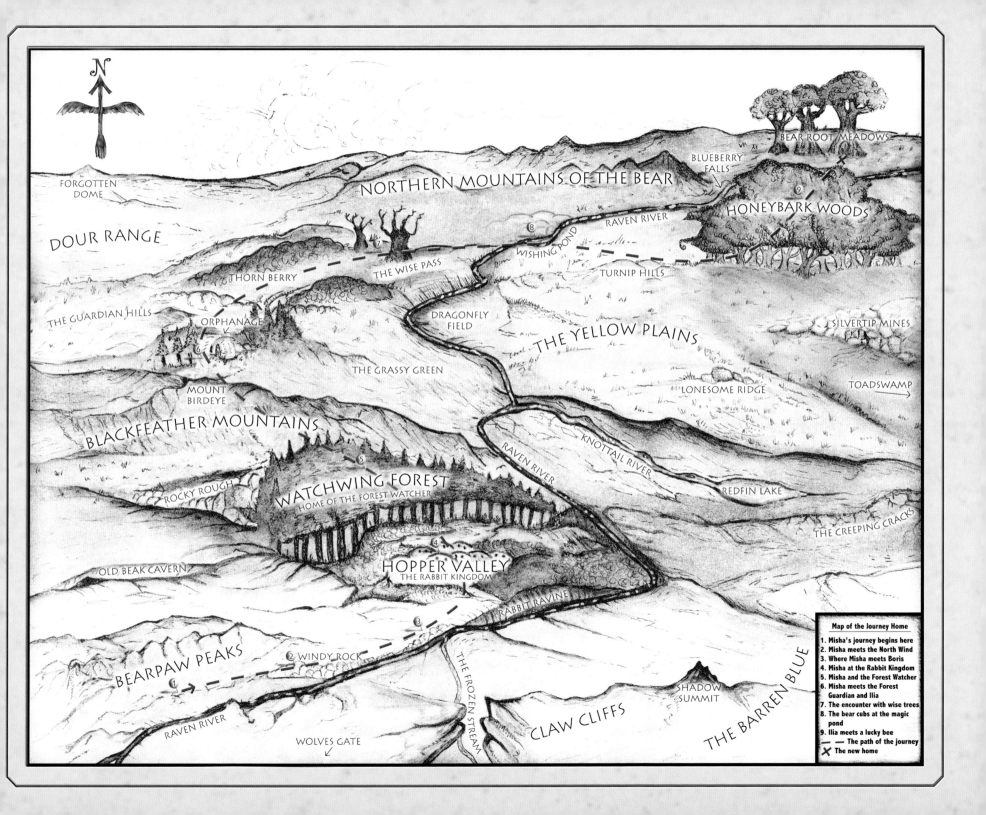

N

FORGOTTEN DOME

DOUR RANGE

NORTHERN MOUNTAINS OF THE BEAR

BLUEBERRY FALLS

BEAR ROOT MEADOWS

HONEYBARK WOODS

9

THORN BERRY

THE WISE PASS

8

WISHING POND

RAVEN RIVER

TURNIP HILLS

THE GUARDIAN HILLS

ORPHANAGE

6

DRAGONFLY FIELD

THE YELLOW PLAINS

SILVERTIP MINES

MOUNT BIRDEYE

THE GRASSY GREEN

LONESOME RIDGE

TOADSWAMP

BLACKFEATHER MOUNTAINS

ROCKY ROUGH

5

WATCHWING FOREST
HOME OF THE FOREST WATCHER

RAVEN RIVER

KNOTTAIL RIVER

REDFIN LAKE

THE CREEPING CRACKS

OLD BEAK CAVERN

4

HOPPER VALLEY
THE RABBIT KINGDOM

RABBIT RAVINE

3

2 WINDY ROCK

BEARPAW PEAKS

1

SHADOW SUMMIT

THE FROZEN STREAM

CLAW CLIFFS

THE BARREN BLUE

RAVEN RIVER

WOLVES GATE

Map of the Journey Home
1. Misha's journey begins here
2. Misha meets the North Wind
3. Where Misha meets Boris
4. Misha at the Rabbit Kingdom
5. Misha and the Forest Watcher
6. Misha meets the Forest Guardian and Ilia
7. The encounter with wise trees
8. The bear cubs at the magic pond
9. Ilia meets a lucky bee
— — The path of the journey
✕ The new home

In a faraway land where the sky meets the mountains and the snow falls, there lived a bear cub named Misha. One day Misha and his mother were traveling through the forest to their winter cave, since autumn was coming to an end. After a while, they stopped by a creek to rest and drink the cool water. Misha ran along the bank and played among the damp vines and roots. Time passed by and Misha went back to be with his mother but she was nowhere to be seen. Panic began to well up within him and he was suddenly very alone. It was oddly quiet and Misha felt as if shadows were surrounding him. He stood next to the gently flowing creek looking in every direction for his mother. Misha called for her, his voice trailing off into the silence. He peered up at the sky, puffy white clouds were thickening as winds blew and snowflakes were falling almost unnoticed. A tear found its way down his cheek.

A winter storm was getting closer making Misha extremely cold and scared. He wandered over the frosty ground searching for his mother. The snowfall grew thicker, was a blizzard on the way? Glancing to the side, he thought he saw his mother's skirt blowing. He ran to her only to find the swirling wind. Had it meant to be so cruel and tricky? Surely, she will find me, Misha thought, as he searched for her.

Snow blanketed the forest floor and an icy chill penetrated the air. Misha wanted to run in every direction at once. He called again for his mother, his cries echoing in the forest. The wind started to wail. Gusts of snow encircled Misha, covering his fur. This must be the North Wind, he thought, shivering. Had the wind blinded his mother? Was she lost in the snow? She had once told him a legend about the North Wind blowing in storms and blinding travelers. Misha noticed an outcropping of rocks ahead so he climbed there to look around.

Standing at the top of the rocks, the cold North Wind came swirling close to Misha and whispered in his ear, Do you think the snow soft and pretty?

Misha paused. There was a calm in the forest and snowflakes were now falling gently. They were soft, and yes, pretty.

In hushed tones the North Wind said, Do you want to see a land of eternal white? Always soft and pretty.

Misha felt dreamy, was there a place for him in this land of white? For a moment, he wanted to go so he would no longer feel lost. Then he thought of his mother. Please help me find my mother, North Wind, cried Misha.

The North Wind let forth a frigid howl, Your mother 's gone, and you will never find her!

Misha stood stunned, were the words truthful or just lies?

In a sudden gust the North Wind transformed into a wispy cloud. Misha looked around to see where the mighty wind had gone, but not even a breeze was felt. The storm had cleared leaving behind only a thin haze. Misha could now see a group of trees so he went there to sit and rest.

He heard something move! Was it the wind again? He eased closer to see what had made the noise. Out hopped a rabbit from behind a tree.

Who are you? Misha asked.

I 'm Boris, said the rabbit.   You look sad. Are you lost in the forest?

Misha's lower lip quivered, Yes, I 'm lost and looking for my mother. Have you seen her?

Boris had not seen her, but invited Misha home to Hopper Valley. Perhaps the Elders of the Rabbit Kingdom could help him. So off they went into the cold winter's day.

Boris led Misha down a hidden path until they came upon some thick undergrowth that led to a snow-covered village. Misha was amazed as curious rabbits began to gather around. The Elders moved forward and introduced the King and Queen of their kingdom. Misha told them about losing his mother in the forest and how he had met Boris.

The Queen of the Rabbits greeted Misha, Stay with us and have a lovely carrot soup for supper.

King Rabbit then warned, Time is getting late, soon the wolves will roam under the moon.

I have to find my mother, Misha said, though his mouth watered at the prospect of hot soup.

Dear Misha, replied The Rabbit Queen, stay with us tonight, have some soup, and then tomorrow in the light of morning we will help you find the Forest Watcher. The Forest Watcher is the Great Raven of wisdom and knowledge who knows all in the forest. The Watcher of the gate and the protector of fate.

As Misha lay in Boris' room that night in a cozy bed under a warm quilt, he thought about his mother and his long day. He nodded off to sleep, the hot soup and the toil of his journey had made him drowsy.

In the light of the next morning, Misha ate breakfast with the rabbits. The King of the Rabbits handed Misha a map made of bark and said, This will help you on your journey. Remember to never give up. You must have faith to find the Forest Watcher. To see him, you must believe in him.

Clutching the map, Misha set off to find his fate. The birch bark felt smooth to his paw and the painted symbols seemed to have a magical glow. He walked a long way until he came to a vast forest filled with thick fog. The trees had sinister shadows that watched him. Misha felt afraid. What would the Forest Watcher be like? Would he really help him? Was he kind hearted? Hesitantly, he made his way through the trees until he reached the edge of a shaded glen. He realized he could no longer see the sky because there was a thick canopy of branches. According to the map, this was the place. He summoned courage then stepped into the glen but there was no Forest Watcher to be seen. Feeling weary Misha climbed onto a rock and was overcome by sadness. A brush against his fur startled him, looking up he came face to face with a quick set of eyes.

The Forest Watcher was more magnificent than he had imagined.

Welcome to Watchwing Forest, Misha. You have met your fears and have a heart of courage. I was here all along watching and waiting. After you met your fears, you could see me. We will travel to the Forest Guardian who will take care of you, the wise Forest Watcher explained.

Forest Guardian? Misha asked, noticing the map had vanished and feeling a bit puzzled.

There is a cave of comfort over the ridge and across the valley. She cares for the orphans of the forest. We must travel quickly if we are to get there today before the darkness overtakes us, the Forest Watcher spoke to Misha.

They started on their journey across the Blackfeather Mountains, the Great Raven guiding and guarding their way. As they traveled, Misha could see the Raven's dark iridescent feathers shining in the sunlight. Their travels went fast and somehow Misha was not tired.

They arrived before nightfall. The Raven lit down to introduce Misha to the waiting Forest Guardian.

Welcome Misha, she greeted him, I am so glad you have arrived, my little friend. The other children are waiting inside to meet you.

Misha timidly peered inside before he entered the cave. There were several little smiling faces. Misha discovered he was not the only one to have been lost.

He turned, and in the distance caught a glimpse of the Forest Watcher flying above the horizon. A gentle arm guided him into the warmth of the cave. If only his heart could be warmed as easily.

After a dinner of turnip stew and huckleberry pie, the children in the Forest Guardian's care sang evening songs and heard enchanting stories. One story was about the Fairy Duster, who comes at bedtime sprinkling magic dust in children's eyes to make them sleepy. Misha had never heard of such fantastic stories. The Forest Guardian read and, as with the wind, Misha felt dreamy again. At bedtime, when the last candle had burnt out, Misha waited to see the Fairy Duster. He waited until his eyelids grew heavy and finally sleep came. In his dreams that night, his mother came to him. She called to him and comforted him. She told Misha not to worry about her, to be strong, for she was in heaven.

Upon waking, he could not remember seeing the Fairy Duster, but visions of his mother comforted him. At breakfast, Misha met Ilia, a little blond bear cub, that had also been lost. After eating, they went out to play, and told stories of how they had come to be with the Forest Guardian. Ilia had been a baby when the Forest Guardian found him in a patch of heartsease flowers, wrapped in a woolen blanket. In the cave of comfort the days slipped by. Misha and Ilia became friends in the play yard of many memories.

Peering out across the land, the Forest Watcher sat at the top of the tallest tree in Watchwing Forest. In his profound knowledge, he was aware of a family that had a place in their hearts for Misha and Ilia. The Great Raven set forth on a swift journey to meet this family. After some time he arrived at their home, a giant gnarled tree. Over blueberry tea, the Raven and the couple discussed the two little bear cubs. The couple rejoiced to adopt the little cubs. Plans were made for a journey in the early spring when weather would permit travel.

When the snow had melted the couple traveled from their home in Bear Root Meadows. They went through Honeybark Woods, across Turnip Hills and Raven River to the orphanage. Misha and Ilia were nervous, but excited, to meet their new parents. Their joy overcame all fears as everyone hugged. That night the new family slept at the cave before starting their journey home the next day.

The sun rose on a new day over Guardian Hills. After a hot breakfast of porridge, the Forest Guardian was busy preparing the family sacks of lunch for their long day ahead. She hugged them all goodbye and gave them a blessing to send them on their way. The new family made their way up the winding path toward the sunrise. The long walk home was a journey of the heart, mind, and soul.

The Forest Guardian felt sad to see them go. She would miss their presence at the fireside where she told her magical stories. Standing to wave farewell, she saw the Forest Watcher perched on a branch. As the Forest Watcher flew away, his shadow faded, dancing in the early morning mist.

The new family traveled until they found a blackberry thicket. They were hungry, so in the cool shade they ate the lunch that the Forest Guardian had packed for them, barley bread with sweet plum jam, wild honey cookies, and crabapple cider. To go with the lunch, the bears picked blackberries until their tummies were full. Misha and Ilia wanted to find the biggest, ripest, and juiciest berries. Near the top of the thicket, they noticed a beautiful dragonfly. They watched it land on the leaves then flutter back into the air, its wings sparkling in the sunshine. They followed the dragonfly to the end of the berry patch and what they saw mesmerized them.

Standing before them were two mysterious ancient trees. The trees had faces that were weathered and friendly, the bear cubs did not want to run, rather they felt drawn to the trees.

The largest tree spoke in a creaking voice, Hello bear cubs, were the berries good?

You talk! Misha managed to say.

We are the Craggytrees of Wise Pass that stand tall and never fall. It 's been ever so long since we had someone to talk to, besides the bugs that buzz our blossoms, the largest tree replied.

How long have you been here? Ilia asked.

A long, long time. We have seen many generations come and go. Many moons and stars have lighted our nights, the tree crackled.   We know you both have a new family. Listen to my words for they are few. Your lives will be filled with wonder, yet there will be times of challenge. Do not be afraid. The moon changes in cycles, as you will. However, your family will be there with you through the changes. What is in your soul is what is important. Now, run back to your parents, they will be looking for you.

Misha and Ilia ran back to their new mother and father. At first, they were not brave enough to tell them they had been talking to trees. However, Misha remembered the Forest Watcher praising him for having a heart of courage, he knew they must tell their story and they did just that.

They had to travel a long distance that day. On their journey they went, full from lunch and blackberries. Along the path father bear spied a waterhole. As Misha and Ilia approached the crystal water, sparkles of light shot up from the surface. It felt good to wade in the cool, clear water. They tried to catch the sparkles of light. A big green toad sat on a moss-covered rock watching Misha and Ilia.

Bear Cubs, the toad called out, make a wish. No one leaves without a wish.

The bear cubs looked at each other and could not help smiling, they had the same wish.

We want to go home! the bear cubs both shouted.

They knew it was time to finish their journey.

The family was close to home. Their parents told them about how life would be, making friends, and the little one-room schoolhouse where they would go to school. They were so excited about their new life and all the things they would see. A honeybee buzzed around Ilia's head, landing on his paw. He knew this meant there must be honey nearby. Mother Bear looked back at Ilia, she took this as a sign of good fortune and that their life together would be good. The bee flew up to the hollow in the tree, where the honey must be. There are things that mothers store away in their hearts. This was one such treasure.

The bear cubs loved their house on the hill. There was always the sound of songbirds in the air. Everyday they walked to the schoolhouse in the meadow. One day, on the way to school, they thought they saw a big dark bird flying above the treetops. The bird flew up into the glare of the sun and the cubs felt a protective presence. Soon the bird had disappeared into the brightness, the Forest Watcher perhaps?

Every evening the bears cooked dinner together. They made fruited pies and honey breads. Mother bear always had soup cooking on the back of the stove. After dinner, the bear cubs asked for stories to be told. Misha and Ilia sometimes thought of the Forest Guardian at story time. They looked for her in their dreams. Their days and dreams were truly enchanted.

The End